THE POKY LITTLE PUPPY COMES TO SESAME STREET

by **Anna H. Dickson** • illustrated by **Tom Brannon**

Featuring Jim Henson's Sesame Street Muppets

 **A GOLDEN BOOK • NEW YORK**
Golden Books Publishing Company, Inc., New York, New York 10106

Published by Golden Books Publishing Company, Inc., in cooperation with Children's Television Workshop

A portion of the money you pay for this book goes to Children's Television Workshop. It is put right back into SESAME STREET and other CTW educational projects. Thanks for helping!

Five little puppies dug a hole under the fence and went off to explore the big city. Down the walk they went, across the street, and up the hill toward the park.

The Poky Little Puppy was last.

Suddenly Poky stopped and stuck his little black nose up in the air. *Sniff, sniff.* He smelled something wonderful.

The Poky Little Puppy scampered around the corner, following his nose.

When four little puppies got to the top of the hill,
they stopped and counted themselves: one, two,
three, four. One little puppy wasn't there.

"Where in the world is that Poky Little Puppy?"
they wondered.

The Poky Little Puppy had found Sesame Street.

Poky ran over and dug a hole under the fence. He
crawled through it to the other side.

Poky saw a cozy place to rest.
He curled up in it and fell fast asleep.

"Somebody is sleeping in my nest!" said Big Bird
when he came home.

Big Bird took Poky to meet his friends. They found Ernie and Bert sitting on the steps of 123 Sesame Street.

"Are you the real Poky Little Puppy?" asked Bert.

"He looks like the Poky Little Puppy to me," said
Ernie.

Poky smiled at them and wagged his tail.

Suddenly the trash can lid flipped open, and Oscar the Grouch popped up.

"I've heard about you," he said. "Aren't you real poky?"

"Oh, yes!" said Grover. "He is that cute and adorable little puppy in the BOOK!"
The Poky Little Puppy wagged his tail again.

Poky's nose twitched. He caught a whiff of
something delicious and ran off to find out what
it was.

"Did you see that?" asked Zoe, as Poky streaked by. "That looked like the Poky Little Puppy," said Elmo. "Only he doesn't seem very poky right now!" Zoe and Elmo decided to follow him.

Poky raced down Sesame Street to Hooper's Store.

In the kitchen, Cookie Monster was taking freshly baked cookies out of the oven.

"Hello, Poky," said Cookie Monster.
"Want a . . . COOOOOKIE?"

So everyone had milk and cookies to celebrate Poky's visit.

"Welcome to Sesame Street, Poky!" his new friends cheered.

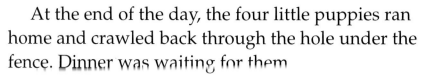

At the end of the day, the four little puppies ran home and crawled back through the hole under the fence. Dinner was waiting for them.

"Where in the world is that Poky Little Puppy?" they asked.

Just as they were finishing their rice pudding, Poky straggled in.

"You missed digging in the sandbox in the park," said his brother.

"You missed dinner—and dessert," said his sister. "You missed all the fun. What a pity you're so poky!"

But the Poky Little Puppy just smiled and curled
up on his own little bed and fell fast asleep.